MY RUSSIAN BABUSHKA, my mother's mother, shared so many things with me and only me, it seemed.

That katydids outgrow their skins and walk right out of them.

That stars make a faint hissing sound on hot summer nights.

That monarch butterflies free themselves from brown chrysalises to become gossamer beings of the air.

Babushka shared a dab of vanilla behind both her and my ears when we baked in the kitchen, so we would "smell delicious," and shared her lap whenever I needed a story.

To the amazing friends and neighbors of my childhood
on Ocean View Drive

PATRICIA LEE GAUCH, EDITOR

G. P. Putnam's Sons
an imprint of Penguin Random House LLC
375 Hudson Street, New York, NY 10014

Library of Congress Cataloging-in-Publication Data is available upon request.
Manufactured in China by RR Donnelley Asia Printing Solutions Ltd.
ISBN 9781524739485
1 3 5 7 9 10 8 6 4 2

Design by Semadar Megged. ◆ Text set in 14.5-point Adobe Jenson Pro.
The illustrations are rendered in pencils and markers.

PATRICIA POLACCO

HOLES IN THE SKY

G. P. Putnam's Sons

One night, it was too hot to sleep in my grandmother's house, so we carried our blankets out to the yard, a custom my babushka brought from her village in Russia—Babushka, my brother, and I all on the same blanket.

We gazed up at the stars.

"You both know what those stars really are, don't you? Holes in the sky. The light of heaven is showing through them from the other side."

Richie and I looked at each other. "What are the holes for?" I asked.

"They are the way into heaven. When it's our time, we all must leave this earth. That's where we go. To the other side."

What Richie and I didn't know was that it was almost Babushka's time. She was ill, and had managed to keep this a secret from us.

"Soon I must go there, but I'll be watching over you both through those holes each and every night," she told us. "I'll send you a sign so you'll know."

It wasn't more than a month later that my beloved babushka went through those holes. Even though she had tried to prepare us, I was devastated. There would never be another Babushka.

Soon after, Grampa sold our farm! He was going to live with Uncle George in Indiana. Mom got a teaching job way out in California, and we were moving there.

The drive took three days. As we crossed the desert at night, I'd look up at the dazzling array of stars that crowded the skies. I found myself whispering, "Please, Babush, you promised. Give me a sign you're there."

Almost as soon as we arrived in Oakland, a Realtor found us the perfect house and Mom bought it. It was a huge old brown shingle place at the crest of a steep hill on Ocean View Drive. From the front porch, we could see the Bay Bridge and, beyond it, the Golden Gate Bridge. (Funny thing, it wasn't golden at all. It was actually orange.)

But what I noticed after the bridges was that our lawn and the lawns of all of the other houses up and down the street were brown and dried up. Dead!

"The drought!" the Realtor said. "We badly need rain. No one is even allowed to water outside with a sprinkler or hose." Shaking her head, the Realtor opened the front door and let us in.

It was sunny and friendly. It instantly felt like home. Mom and Richie and I all had our own rooms. I discovered a small window in my closet that pushed open to reveal a clear view of the sky.

That first night, I stood on a chair, opened the window, and whispered to my babushka, "I miss you so much. I need that sign, Bubbie." But it didn't come.

One day, there was a loud knock at my front door. When I answered it, a boy was standing there with a paper basket full of freshly picked flowers. I wondered where they'd come from, with the drought and all. I had never seen anyone like him up close before. He had brown skin and curly black hair that framed his face.

"Wanna buy a May basket?" he asked through a toothy grin.

I looked at him for a long time.

"It ain't May!" I said sternly. He completely ignored my observation.

"The O'Learys used to live here. . . . What have you guys done to the place?"

"See for yourself!" I snapped as I motioned him in.

"Name's Stewart. Live right up the block," he chirped as he went from room to room. I was fascinated by him, so I just followed him and listened.

When we got to the refrigerator and he had examined just about everything in it, he noticed the art table. "Hey, look. You have a ton of paper. We could make thousands of May baskets." He took a seat and grabbed a pair of scissors. I was so curious about him, I just sat down and started making May baskets, too.

We must have made ten baskets, easy. I didn't have the heart to ask where he'd gotten flowers, or where we'd get ours. I didn't need to. We filled Stewart's wagon, and he walked me up to his own house! His lawn was brown like everyone else's, but there in his front yard was a string of rosebushes.

"We use buckets of water we've saved from the washing machine and sinks to water these flowers," he said. He must have read my mind.

We picked enough flowers to fill our paper baskets, then began to amble down the block, selling them at every house. My new neighbors weren't like the folks back home. In Michigan, pretty much everyone looked alike. Here, people were so different.

Across the street was the Martinez family from Mexico. Next to them, the Zydans from Yemen. Then the Vartarians, an Armenian family, who owned a restaurant on College Avenue. The Cho family had a gift shop on the corner. On the other corner was a black Muslim bakery that Stewart said made the biggest and best cookies in the whole world.

We'd sold almost all our baskets and were making our way back to Ocean View when we passed a house that Stewart took me across the street to pass. The yard looked like a jungle, dark and buried in dusty brown vines and tall weeds. I almost couldn't see the house!

"Ole lady Bacci's place," he hissed. "She's mean to all us kids. Calls the police when we play stickball in the street near her house." I saw the curtains part slightly and knew that the lady inside was watching us.

We bought ice cream for a bunch of kids in the neighborhood with what we'd earned and finally called it a day, the best day ever.

That night, before bed, I looked up at the stars from my little window. "Babushka," I whispered, "I met the greatest kid today, you'd just love him."

Then I sighed and watched the sky for a sign from her. But there was no sign.

Stewart and I became BEST FRIENDS. I learned that he had three sisters and a younger brother, a mom and dad who worked, and a grandmother, Miss Eula, who took care of the kids and the house—and whom everyone in the neighborhood just loved. I sure wanted to meet her.

Then one day, Stewart came over and said his grandmother wanted to meet me!

The moment we walked into her kitchen, it smelled like my bubbie's kitchen, the air heavy with the aroma of freshly baked bread and the sweet scent of sugar cookies.

Just as we rounded the corner, there she was! Eula Mae Walker, standing with her back to us, stirring a crock pot on a sturdy cast-iron woodstove. Just like my bubbie's back home.

"Grandmommie, she's here. The girl I've been telling you about,"
Stewart said.

Miss Eula turned and looked right at me. "Grinnell," she sang out.

"My middle name," he whispered.

"So this is that child," she cried.

"This is her!" Stewart announced, motioning toward me.

"Well, baby dear," she said, "you come right over here and let me give
you some sugar!"

Then she threw open her arms and I jumped into her hug. Her ample
embrace wrapped completely around me and lifted me clean off the floor.
I didn't ever want to let go.

"Grinnell tells me that you two met because of flowers." I nodded
and grinned at Stewart. "Did he tell you about my secret garden?"
I gave Stewart a puzzled look. "It would give me pleasure to show
it to you myself." She smiled as she led us out to the back
porch, where we stepped into Miss Eula's glorious garden.

It looked like something out of a storybook. Enormous rosebushes, cluttered with giant blooms, gave a wondrous perfume to the air around us; resplendent bougainvilleas trailed completely around the fence. There were birdbaths everywhere, full of fluttering sparrows, splashing water as they drenched their little heads. The yard was alive with flitting butterflies and hummingbirds drinking from a cascading wisteria. I was breathless.

On the back porch stood dozens of buckets. Miss Eula saw me looking. "That's how we keep these flowers healthy, by pouring gray water on them every day—bathwater, washing machine and even dishwater." I could hardly take in all of the beauty.

"You know, baby dears, there was another backyard garden on this block that was even more beautiful than this one."

I could see Stewart already knew the answer.

"Verna Bacci's," Miss Eula said.

"That mean old crab," Stewart mumbled. "Her yard sure looks awful now. So full of dry weeds and brambles and vines, you can barely see the house."

Miss Eula thought for a moment. "Verna was my best friend, still is, really. But since her son Angelo died, she hasn't been the same."

"I didn't even know she had a son," Stewart blurted out.

"She and I planted our gardens at just about the same time." Miss Eula tugged at an unwanted weed that was intruding into her hostas. "We helped each other. Her garden was magnificent. Gorgeous. It looked like something out of Italy. A fountain, statues, and a lovely grape arbor with a huge friendly table under it, where we feasted on her wonderful Italian cooking."

"She and her son Angelo spent hours and hours making it look as beautiful as it was—he was going to be a landscape gardener when he grew up. He was lost in a terrible accident. I expect seeing all of you children laughing and playing is a constant reminder that her child is gone."

"No wonder she's so mean," I whispered. "She must be lonely."

All of us thought for a time.

"Maybe if we do something really nice for her, she'll know that all of us care and that she's not alone," I said suddenly.

"Maybe we could clean up her yard and bring her garden back to life!" Stewart offered.

"In this drought? That'd take a miracle!"

"Oh, baby dears," Miss Eula said, "miracles are everywhere. They're all around us, just waiting to jump up!"

I caught my breath. My bubbie used to say that exact same thing.

"I think, Grinnell, you have a wonderful idea. Wonderful!" Miss Eula crowed. She slapped her chest and laughed from a deep holy place inside. "Let's see, now," she said. "Verna is going to visit her sister in Fresno in just a few days. She'll leave her house key with me, as always. Maybe that's the time to make this miracle happen."

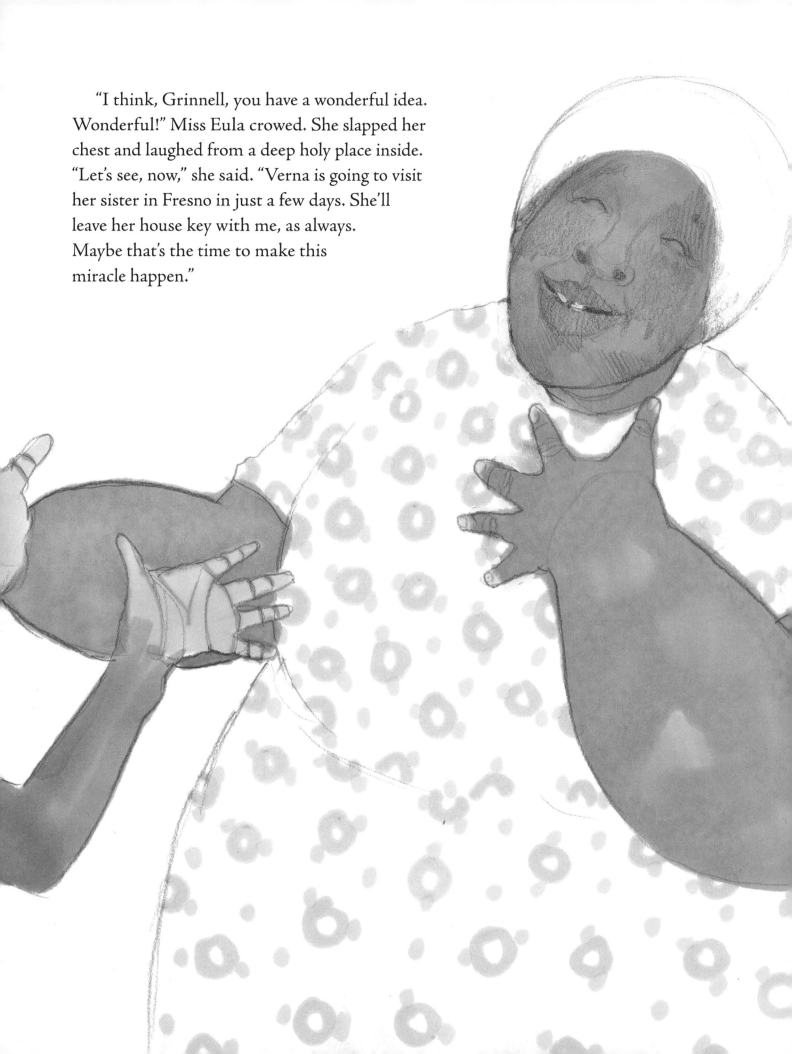

Sure enough, it was. By the time Mrs. Bacci left for her sister's, Miss Eula'd gotten everyone on the block to jump in and help bring Mrs. Bacci's garden back to life. They started in the backyard. She knew where everything had once been, so she bustled from here to there, directing the neighbors where to slash, where to dig, and where to prune.

Miss Eula was everywhere!

And everyone worked their heads off—the McCalls, the Greers, the Heinleins, the Kodinskis—pulling dead weeds, culling shrubs, setting roses free from their tangled vines. The Krebs girls helped Stewart and me find a koi pond that was knee-deep in mud. We all cheered when we unearthed the grape arbor—and the table! The Zydans hauled truckloads of debris and cuttings off to the dump.

"Oh, darlings . . . good work . . . good work!" Miss Eula cooed to each of us.

It took four days to clean up. Now for transplanting the flowers and shrubs that everyone had donated! Miss Eula oversaw it all. She knew which plants needed sun, which needed shade, and which needed both.

"Okay, darlings," she shouted out. "Now we have to water all of this." I couldn't even guess how, but she organized it on the spot. It wasn't long before the entire neighborhood started bringing water they could spare in buckets and jars and containers. It was a sight to see!

That night, I watched the stars from my window.
I felt like my bubbie was closer than ever. I knew
she'd be proud that I had worked so hard to make
someone else happy. I was just sure the sign would come,
but no sign came, not a spark nor a shimmer.

It wasn't long, with the neighbors watering those plants by
the day, before the bright green of tender new growth appeared
on every single bush, plant, and shrub. Some of the fathers even
repainted the red trim on Mrs. Bacci's house.

But when Mrs. Bacci got home, no one heard from her. Not even
Miss Eula.

Then one overcast day, I was at Miss Eula's house when she got an urgent call from Mrs. Bacci. "Come with me, baby dears, sounds like she needs us."

When we arrived in Mrs. Bacci's back garden, she was kneeling in the middle of her courtyard under the grape arbor. Sobbing.

"You had no right, Eula. No right," she choked out.

Stewart and I couldn't understand.

"Eula, you know why I let the garden die—because Angelo did. It was his garden and I couldn't bear to see it anymore." She sobbed even harder.

Miss Eula knelt next to her. "But, Verna, Angelo would want you to keep his garden. He loved it so. Wouldn't it be the perfect tribute to him?"

But she didn't have a chance to answer, because a second miracle jumped up. With all of us standing right there together, a light mist started to settle over the garden, then fine droplets fell from the sky. I couldn't believe it.

"It's rain, Grandmommie . . . it's rain," Stewart crowed.

Miss Eula pulled Mrs. Bacci to her feet and took her hand. Then Miss Eula took mine and I took Stewart's and he took Mrs. Bacci's, and with rain pouring down now, we started to circle—the four of us together—with our faces to the sky.

"Angelo's letting us know that he wants this garden, Verna, and he wants you to flourish in it," Miss Eula whispered softly.

That day, I found myself wondering why Mrs. Bacci got her sign from Angelo but my bubbie hadn't sent me mine.

That night, Stewart and I were in Miss Eula's kitchen, helping her wash up the dinner dishes. As Miss Eula and I stood at her sink, we peered out the window at the dazzling array of stars twinkling above us.

"Look at them, will you, baby dear? Look how bright," Miss Eula whispered.

I nodded as I gazed up at them.

"Do you know what those really are?" she asked quietly. "Those are holes in the sky. The light of heaven shining through from the other side. All of those we love who have left us have moved through them and watch over us."

I gasped. I hadn't ever told Miss Eula that secret from my bubbie. Was that the sign? Miss Eula hugged me close, then trundled over to her woodstove and reached for something on the shelf above it. A small bottle of vanilla! She opened it and dabbed some behind each ear. Then she did the same to me. "Now we both smell delicious, don't we, baby dear?"

There it was! The sign from Bubbie. It was in front of me all along. Not in the sky alone, but in Miss Eula herself.

From that time on, Miss Eula shared so many things with me.
Her lap would always welcome me whenever I needed her
comfort and wisdom. (Her ample neck was a warm place to nestle.)
Her grace under fire, which seemed so effortless, touched
everyone around her, including me. She wore her dignity like a
queenly robe and jeweled crown.
And she taught me . . .

that all things reach for the stars. Even us.